Sarah Noble Ives

Songs of the Shining Way

Sarah Noble Ives

Songs of the Shining Way

ISBN/EAN: 9783744771818

Printed in Europe, USA, Canada, Australia, Japan

Cover: Foto ©Andreas Hilbeck / pixelio.de

More available books at **www.hansebooks.com**

Songs
of the
Shining Way.

SONGS OF THE SHINING WAY

~ BY SARAH NOBLE-IVES ~

~ WITH PICTURES BY THE AUTHOR ~

NEW YORK
R. H. RUSSELL
1899

TO EDNA CHAFFEE NOBLE.

FOR her who dared to take the girl
    Half-formed and careless to
        her heart,
I write these simple childish
        rhymes,
    That she may have that early
        part,
The baby that she might not see,
The childhood fancies missed in
        me.

S. N. L.

Contents

ON THE SHINING WAY

ALL through the happy Child-
hood land
They travel the Shining
Way,
The children fresh from the dawn of
life,
With never a thought but play.

There's never a care 'neath the shin-
ing hair
Where the sunrise stores its beams;
The wind that blows is the wind of
morn
From the shore of the Sea of
Dreams.

There's no other way so glad and sweet,
And no other sky so blue,
And the joy of the road to the children is
That nothing but dreams come true.

There are great dream meadows and purple hills
That only the children know;
They can tell where the tall dream cities rise,
And the sweet dream flowers grow.

So on they pass by the milestone years,
    To the land where the grown folks stay,
And only once is the journey made
    On the wonderful Shining Way.

The Beginning.

H ERE is the beginning of
the road;
And it's morning on the
hill-top in the sky;
And there's mist across the valley
to hide the Shining Way,
That's full of other children and
happy hours of play,
Where Dorothy will travel by
and by.

The air is full of voices strange and sweet,
That crowd around her cradle as it swings.
She thinks they're made of something white that shimmers on the grass,
For she doesn't know a dew-drop from the bobolinks that pass,
And she doesn't know a host of other things.

ON THE SHINING WAY.

First Stage
OS
The Journey.

SING ho! for the road that
    opens down
      Out of the sleepy old Baby
      Town.
Sing ho! for the joy of the Shining
    Way,
For Dorothy took her first steps to-
    day.

Mother has helped her alone to
    stand,
And now she is holding her dimpled
    hand,
And now there's a start and a tipsy
    run,
And life on the road is well begun.

There's a tear in the midst of Mother's smiles,
But Mother will lead her the first few miles.
So let her start on her journey gay.
Sing ho! for the joy of the Shining Way.

An Early Start.

THE dark had not un-
wrapped the skies
When I awoke, and
rubbed my eyes.
The world was full of chirping
birds,
I heard their soft, half-sleepy
words.
I tiptoed softly on the floor,
I slipped the bolt, stole thro' the
door,
And lo! a wondrous world of gray
And silver mist before me lay.
The white dews wet my small
bare feet,
As I ran thro' the meadows, sweet
With clover nodding all about,
And sleepy hum-bees creeping out.

And then a strange thing came to
pass;
The Sun was sleeping in the grass;
He must have wakened when I
came,
For all at once a rosy flame
Peeped at me o'er a little mound,
And soon the bright Sun, warm
and round

ON THE SHINING WAY.

Noble-Ives.

15

Was looking at me, smiling down
To see my little slumber-gown.

O fair the meadow was to see
The blossoms laughed and spoke to me;
And drops like pearls in every place
Were hanging on the spider's lace;
And little rainbows everywhere
Were dancing in the golden air;
And bees, and yellow butterflies,
And beetles, brown and big and wise,
Went buzzing, flying all about,
And busy ants ran in and out,
And songs were in the deep-blue sky,
—I could not see, they flew so high.

But all about these things I know,
Because the daisies whispered low,
And told me all they knew—much more
Than I had ever dreamed before.

And broad and white across the day
Before me ran the Shining Way.

The Butter-fly.

BUTTERFLY, say, is it true,
 All that the daisies have told?
 Are those bright spots on your wings
Made out of rainbows and gold?
Did you come down on a beam
 Of light that shot thro' the blue?
Are you a piece of the sun?
 Butterfly, say, is it true?

The Moon.

SWIM, white Moon, in the dusky blue,
  Swim in the still dark sky.
Soft are the clouds that cover you;
  And Jimmy and Alice and I
Some time, perhaps, a journey will make
Across the sea on your silver wake.

Swing, white Moon, to the breeze that blows
  From the Milky Way so bright.
Alice told me (and Alice knows),
  That I may climb up some night,
And swing in the cradle you make for me,
Higher than even the highest tree.

ON THE SHINING WAY.

DOWN by the side of the Shining Way
    There's a ship on the raging sea;
  And she's bearing a rich and royal
      load
  Over the waves to me.

(There are cherries juicy and red and sweet,)
    And when she has reached this side
The cargo's mine, and the ship returns
    To Jimmy across the tide.

If I blow right hard from my side of the sea
    She steadily keeps her track;
And when she has travelled too far for me,
Jimmy will blow her back.

WE were tired of travel
    one afternoon,
        And stopped at the sign
of "The Great Barn-Door,"
And Jimmy and Alice took rooms in the loft,
    While I had mine on the second floor.

Jimmy and Alice went climbing high
    Over the rafters above my head,
And peeped thro' the swallow-holes out at the
        sky.
    —If Mother had seen them, what would she
        have said?

But I stayed down in the soft new hay,
    And the sun crept in thro' a yellow chink,
And a long beam found me out where I lay,
    And tickled my eyes till it made them blink.

The dust-motes circled and whirled and danced,
  And my pillow was soft and warm and deep,
And the hay smelled sweet, and it somehow chanced
  That there in the mow I feel asleep.

And I dreamed a dream full of swallows' wings,
  And elfish motes in the dusty air,
And thousands of other wonderful things;
  Till Jimmy and Alice found me there.

By Coach.

W E'RE traveling hard and fast to-day,—
    Jimmy and Alice and me—
Bowling along on the Shining Way,
    With a royal coach and three.

We laugh at the folk who are passing by,
    Dragging their weary feet
Deep in the dust that our whizzing wheels
    Have raised in the flying street.

Fields and forests flit out of sight;
    And if all goes just as we planned
We'll travel on till we reach the bars
    At the entrance to Fairy Land.

And what is the coach on our lordly quest?
    And where are the foaming three?
Why, the coach is the dump-cart, and the rest—
    Just Jimmy and Alice and me.

THRO' FAIRY LAND

IT was dark when we stopped at the Fairy-Land bars,
And over our heads there were millions of stars;
And I was quite frightened, but Jimmy looked bold,
And Alice just shivered—she said it was cold.

We timidly knocked, and then, just as I feared
They would not let us in, lo' the bars disappeared,
And the stars dropped right down from the sky, and behold!
Each one was a lamp for a fairy to hold.

And the fairies went dancing like leaves in the wind,
And beckoned to us as we crept on behind;
And queer little faces, brimful of surprise,
Looked out of the darkness with queer little eyes.

But O the sweet fairies! I never could tell
Of the rose-hues we saw in that wonderful dell—
The daffodil-yellow, the purple and green,
But the sweetest of all was the lily-white Queen.

They sang of the land of the Sugary Dews,
Where children may eat a whole pie, if they choose;
A wonderful land, which some day we shall see,
If the Shining Way leads us—Jim, Alice and me.

O we shouted with glee! and then to our surprise
The stars drifted back again into the skies,
The fairies all vanished, I covered my head,—
And when I looked up, we were all three in bed

Bird's-nest Hollow.

ON THE SHINING WAY.

THERE is something puzzles me.—
In the hollow apple-tree,
Where the Shining Way is broadest, there's a nest;
Two fat Robins live in it,
In and out I see them flit,
And the biggest wears a gorgeous crimson vest.

We are friends, and so when I
Come to look, they do not fly,
But they chatter from the branches of the tree;
And I run down there to play,
When the sun shines, every day,
And next year they say they'll build a nest for me.

I peeped in one day, and found
Five small eggs, all blue and round,
And the Robins made me promise not to tell.
For (they said that this was so)
Jim and Alice must not know.
So I promised, and I've kept the secret well.

When to-day I climbed the tree,
  Those two birds had company;
There were five small squirming children in the nest;
  And the Robins whispered me,
  'Twas a case of charity,
For the poor wee birdies were not even dressed.

And those little wriggling things
  Had big mouths, but wore no wings,
And the Robins served refreshments down the row.
  But the eggs are gone, you see;
  That's the thing that puzzles me.
Did those small birds eat them up, I'd like to know?

WE ARE FRIENDS.

A Sorrow.

THE White Rat died last night.
    We found him cold and stiff;
We wrapped him warm and tight.
    In my best handkerchief.

Jimmy marched on before,
    Bearing the poor dead Rat;
Alice deep mourning wore,
    I had papa's silk hat.

Jimmy the sermon preached,
    Alice and I just cried.
That was a noble speech,
    Worthy the Rat that died!

We made him a tiny grave,
  Down in the shadow dim
Where the willow hedge-rows wave
  We solemnly buried him.

Jimmy and Alice and I
  Went sadly back to our play.
But there's a cloud in the sky,
  And a shade on the Shining Way.

THE RAINBOW

STORM-CLOUDS and thunder and
  dark rainy weather,
  Wet streams are flowing all down
    the Shining Way;
Jimmy and Alice and I are here together,
  Cooped in the nursery and longing for a
    play.

Look! there's a sunbeam, through a sky-crack poking;
  Quick! get your shoes off, as still as still can be;
Slip out the back door, Mother isn't looking,
  Steal down the wood-road, before she turns to see.

Great jolly puddles, round and wet and gleaming—
  Here's a still clear one, grassy, cool and sweet;
But we love the brown ones, and in we paddle, screaming,
  Laughing, while the soft mud oozes 'round our feet.

31

Trees shake their wet cloaks, and on us falls a shower;
　We laugh the louder, as down the road we run.
See! there's a cowslip, and here's a fairies' bower,
　All made of violets, nodding to the sun.

Down in the East, where we still can hear the thunder,
　Over the cloud bends a misty, shining Bow.
Right at the foot of it are hidden many wonders,
　If we can get there before the colors go.

Run, hand in hand, then, hair all a-dripping,
　Bare feet splashing thro' the puddles as we fly.
Soft shines the Rainbow, as toward it we are tripping;
　The green earth is waving and smiling to the sky.

HORSE-BACK

JIMMY and Alice and I one day,
　　Were filled with a sudden pride;
No more would we walk on the Shining Way,
　　'Twas pleasanter, far, to ride.

For Billy, the old white horse, was there,
　　He could easily carry three,
And on his back we would gaily fare
　　To the shores of the Sunset Sea.

So up to the orchard fence we tripped,
　　And Billy looked kind and mild,
And on to his back we softly slipped,
　　And Billy, he sort of smiled.

I sat in the middle and clung to Jim,
　　And Alice was out by the tail;
And "Get up, Billy!" we said to him,
　　And away we went in a gale.

But we never got to the Sunset Sea,
    With its fiery waves aglow,
For we didn't count on the old plum-tree,
    And Billy, he did, you know.

Oh, Billy looked kind and mild enough,
    But a plot in his heart did hide;
He knew that the plum-tree bark was rough,
    And the branches were low and wide.

So straight for the tree old Billy steered,
    And vainly we shouted "Whoa!"
His mind was fixed, and he never veered
    From the path where he meant to go.

Under the tree he firmly trod,
    ('Twas just high enough for him,)
And we went tumbling on the sod.
    Scraped off by a scraggly limb.

No more we rode on the Shining Way;
    We were bruised, and our thoughts were sad;
While Billy winked, as he looked our way;
    And his wink was knowing and bad.

An Ocean Voyage

THERE'S an ocean wide we must cross to-day,
  For it stretches across the Shining Way.
    A board will make us a famous boat;
Hurrah! for the high seas. We're afloat!

Alice will pilot across the waves,
Jimmy and I are the galley-slaves,
We bend to the broomstick instead of the oar,
And Alice steers for the further shore.

Carefully on our course we keep
Over the trackless and rolling deep.
Under our vessel slowly swim
Minnows, tadpoles and monsters grim.
(Fishes we know, but have never seen,)
And a bull-frog croaks from the rushes green.

The journey near to an end has grown,
When Alice's rudder strikes a stone.
A lurch—a scramble—a sudden scream,
And over we go in the wet, wet stream.

Alice is dripping, and so am I;
Water has got into Jimmy's eye;
But land is reached—we are safe, though cold.
And we wonder if Mother may chance to scold?

The Dragon fly

WHERE the Shining Way leads on,
  Thro' the garden, o'er the lawn,
  Past the road and down the hill,
There's a place so strange and still,
Nothing like the world we see
Every morning, you and me.
There we found a little pond
Edged with rushes, and beyond
Grow the marshes, green and high.
Wild rice climbing to the sky,

37

Fragrant flag and iris beds
Fringed with purple arrow-heads.

Little moving waves of air
Quiver o'er the grasses fair;
On the shining water blue
Broad round leaves are shining too;
Lilies, dreaming in the sun—
From the bank I peeped in one,
And the petals, wide apart,
Showed a sun within its heart.
And the rushes tall and free,
Like a forest seemed to me,
With the rice-trees waving 'round.
But the silence! Not a sound!
Very still the lilies lay
In the golden summer day.

Sudden, from the wide blue sky,
Whirred a monster Dragon-Fly.
Proudly, all alone he came,
Armor polished to a flame
On his body, and his wings,
Gauzy, wondrous, shining things,
Seemed to catch the water's blue,
And the yellow sunbeams, too.
He's a hermit, and the spot
We had found, it seems, was not

All our own, for here he lives
On the sweet the iris gives,
And each day he sallies forth,
East and west and south and north,
Tilting like a tourney knight,
Putting all his foes to flight.

Never dares a grasshopper
Or a cricket there to stir,
While the water-bugs at play,
When they see him, scud away.
And his duty is to keep
Sentry, while the lilies sleep.
So that every harmful thing,
Bats that bite, and gnats that sting,
Crawling worm and robber bee
From his shining lance must flee.

A HALF for PROVENDER

WE made our little garden-plots before the spring was passed,
And Jimmy, he raised radishes, because they grow so fast;
And Alice planted flower-seeds, to beautify the ground,
But I chose cabbages—they grow so grand and great and round.

And Jimmy's garden flourished—he had a splendid crop,
All round and red below the ground, and broad and green on top.
One day he pulled and ate them all—with salt they're very good—
Then Jimmy gave up gardening—but that is understood.

And Alice's sweet peas and things were beautifully fair,
But Tim, the gardener, smiled one day, to see them growing there,
But what he said was, "Faix, Miss Alice, thim was rare foine sades,
But ye've murthered ivery blissed wan, an' only lift the wades."

Well, cabbage-raising does not pay, my garden is a fright.
There came a Morning-Glory Vine, and like a thief last night
He stole along my pretty rows, and this is what he's done:
He's twined around my cabbage plants, and pulled them every one,
And hung them with their roots to dry, like clothes upon a line—
Just spoiled my little garden-plot—that wicked 'Glory Vine.

And that is why we do not care for gardening to-day;
The crops are very poor this year, and kites are better play.

THRO THE CORNFIELD

THERE'S a forest thro' which we went to-day,
    Waving and green and high,
    With feathery tassels tall and gay
Nodding against the sky;
The place of all others for fairy tales,
    And plays of the years gone by.

And this is the game we children played—
    I was an Ogre grim,
Alice the Princess that fell asleep
    Down in the forest dim,
And the Prince who wakened her with a kiss
    When he found her—that was Jim.

The Prince came riding so proud and bold
    On a prancing corn-stalk steed,
And many a blade was thrust at him,
    But little did Jimmy heed;
And long vines plucked him to hold him back
    From doing that daring deed.

The Ogre leaped from its hiding-place,
    With a menace fierce and grim,
And a big green pumpkin kept the door,
    And scowled and leered at him;
But he bravely charged and routed his foes
    With his trusty "Cherry-Limb."

The corn-blades dropped on their bended joints,
    But vainly for mercy pled,
The pumpkin yielded, the Ogre turned
    With a horrible shriek and fled,
The Princess was duly kissed, and so
    Sweet Alice and Jim were wed.

THE HALO

THERE's a picture of an angel, hanging on our study wall,
   A lovely angel with white wings, and very grand and tall.
   Around about her head there is a shining golden ring,
And I asked Jimmy why she wore that funny yellow thing;
And Jimmy laughed and said to me; "Why, silly, don't you know?
That's nothing but a saint-hole; all angels have them so.

The Shining Way runs through it, straight to her heavenly home,
And when she's tired of the earth, she calls to God to come;
He reaches down and pulls her though, before you can count seven,
And you can't see her any more, because she is in Heaven."

I don't quite understand it, the thought is very new;
But if I had a saint-hole, I'd go to Heaven too.

www.ingramcontent.com/pod-product-compliance
Lightning Source LLC
Chambersburg PA
CBHW022204020726
47496CB00008B/2878